# THE SHADOW IN THE BLACKWOOD MIRROR

GAURAV CHANDRAWANSHI

# Contents


*Preface*                                                    *v*

*Acknowledgements*                                           *vii*

1. The Whispers Start                                        1

2. The Eyes In The Portraits                                 3

3. The Whispering Walls                                      6

4. The Secret Diary                                          10

5. The Ghosts Of Blackwood                                   13

6. Bloodlines                                                17

7. The Mirror Shows All                                      20

8. Trapped In Time                                           23

9. The Wasteland                                             26

10. The Nightmare Factory                                    29

11. Echoes Of The Past                                       33

12. The Sanctuary                                            36

13. Journey Into Darkness                                    39

14. The Gathering Storm                                      42

15. Light's Fury                                             46

16. The Cycle Repeats                                        49

17. Whispers Of The Past                                     51

18. Facing The Shadows                                       54

19. Shattered Reflections                                    57

20. A New Dawn (and A Looming Shadow)                        61

Author's Note                                                63

About the Author                                             65

# Preface

The story you are about to read is not just a story. It is a journey into the heart of darkness, a confrontation with the shadows that lurk within us all. It is a tale of fear, of despair, of the struggle to overcome the monsters that haunt our dreams and the demons that dwell within our souls.

But it is also a story of hope, of courage, of the power of the human spirit to triumph over adversity. It is a story about finding the light within ourselves, even in the darkest of times, and using that light to illuminate the world around us.

This book was born from my own fears, from the nightmares that have haunted me since childhood. It is a reflection of my own journey, my own struggle to confront the darkness and find the strength to overcome it.

But it is also a reflection of the world we live in, a world where darkness often seems to prevail, where fear and hatred cast long shadows over our lives. It is a reminder that we are not alone in our struggles, that there are others who share our fears, our doubts, our anxieties.

And it is a call to action, a plea to find the light within ourselves, to embrace our courage, and to fight back against the darkness that threatens to consume us.

I invite you to join me on this journey, to step into the shadows of Blackwood Manor and confront the creatures that lurk within. But be warned: this is not a story for the faint of heart. It is a story that will challenge you, that will make you question your own beliefs, that will force you to confront your deepest fears.

But if you are brave enough to face the darkness, you will also find the light. You will discover the strength within yourself, the courage to overcome any obstacle, the hope that will guide you through the darkest of times.

So open this book, turn the page, and step into the world of "The Shadow in the Blackwood Mirror." But be prepared to face your own reflection, to confront the shadows that dwell within your soul.

For the darkness is coming. And only the light can save us.

# Acknowledgements

This book would not exist without the unwavering love and support of my family. To my mom, Manisha Chandrawanshi, thank you for nurturing my imagination, for believing in my dreams, and for always being my biggest cheerleader. To my dad, Chandrakishor Chandrawanshi, thank you for your quiet strength, your endless patience, and for teaching me the value of perseverance. And to my sister, Aishwarya Chandrawanshi, thank you for your laughter, your friendship, and for always being there to share the journey.

To my extended family, thank you for your love and encouragement.

To my friends, thank you for the laughter, the adventures, and for always being there to lend an ear or a helping hand.

And to the readers, thank you for taking a chance on this book, for stepping into the shadows of Blackwood Manor and facing the darkness alongside Sarah. I hope this story will stay with you long after you turn the final page.

# CHAPTER ONE

# THE WHISPERS START

Sarah was a writer, but not a very happy one. Her first book hadn't done well. People said it wasn't scary enough. This made Sarah sad. She wanted to write truly scary stories, stories that would make people shiver and hide under their blankets.

One gloomy afternoon, Sarah received a strange letter. It was an invitation to stay at a place called Blackwood Manor. The letter said the manor was old and forgotten, hidden deep in a spooky forest. It also said that the manor had a dark history, full of secrets and maybe even ghosts.

Sarah felt a chill run down her spine. This was exactly the kind of place that could inspire her to write a truly terrifying story! She packed her bags and set off on a journey to Blackwood Manor.

The drive was long and eerie. The forest seemed to press in on the road, its branches like skeletal fingers reaching out to grab her. As the sun began to set, Sarah finally arrived at the manor. It was a massive, imposing structure, with dark windows and crumbling stone walls.

Sarah took a deep breath and stepped inside. The air was thick with dust and the smell of decay. Cobwebs hung like macabre decorations from the high ceilings. A sense of dread washed over her, but Sarah pushed it aside. She was a writer, and this was her chance to face her fears and find the inspiration she needed.

As she explored the manor, Sarah found a hidden room. Inside, there was an old, ornate mirror. As she gazed into its depths, she felt a strange pull, as if the mirror was calling to her. And then, she saw it – a flicker of movement in the reflection, a shadow that wasn't her own.

Sarah gasped and stumbled back. Her heart pounded in her chest. Was it her imagination, or was there something truly sinister lurking within the Blackwood Mirror?

**(To be continued...)**

# CHAPTER TWO

# THE EYES IN THE PORTRAITS

The shadowy figure in the mirror had shaken Sarah to her core. She couldn't shake the feeling that she was being watched, that something malevolent lurked within the depths of Blackwood Manor. But she was determined to be brave, to explore the mysteries of this creepy place. After all, wasn't this the kind of experience that could inspire her to write a truly terrifying tale?

Taking a deep breath, Sarah left the hidden room and ventured further into the manor. The hallway stretched before her, seemingly endless, lined with portraits of stern-faced men and women who seemed to stare down at her with disapproval. As she walked, she couldn't shake the feeling that the eyes in the portraits were following her, their gazes boring into her back.

She entered a grand library, its shelves overflowing with ancient books bound in leather and covered in dust. The air was thick with the smell of old paper and decaying wood. Sarah ran her fingers along the spines of the books, imagining the stories they held within. She felt a strange connection to this place, as if the manor itself was whispering secrets to her.

Suddenly, a loud crash echoed from the floor above. Sarah jumped, her heart pounding. She grabbed a heavy bookend from a nearby shelf, her makeshift weapon offering a small sense of security. Cautiously, she made her way towards the staircase, her footsteps echoing in the eerie silence.

As she ascended the stairs, the feeling of being watched intensified. She could almost hear whispers swirling around her, voices from the past murmuring secrets she couldn't quite decipher. The hair on the back of her neck prickled with a sense of unseen eyes upon her.

She reached the top of the stairs and found herself in a long, dimly lit corridor. The doors lining the hallway were all closed, each one concealing unknown mysteries. Sarah hesitated, unsure which way to go. Then, she noticed a faint light emanating from under one of the doors.

With a mixture of fear and curiosity, Sarah crept towards the door. She slowly turned the handle, the rusty hinges groaning in protest. The door creaked open, revealing a small, dusty bedroom. A single candle flickered on the nightstand, casting long, dancing shadows on the walls.

And then, Sarah saw it. Sitting on the edge of the bed, bathed in the flickering candlelight, was a figure. It was a woman, dressed in a long, white gown. Her back was to Sarah, but Sarah could see her long, dark hair cascading down her shoulders.

Sarah's breath caught in her throat. Was this a ghost? A figment of her imagination? Or something even more sinister? She took a step forward, wanting a closer look.

The woman slowly turned her head, and Sarah gasped. The woman's face was pale and gaunt, her eyes hollow and black. But it was her mouth that truly horrified Sarah. It was stretched into a wide, grotesque grin, revealing rows of sharp, pointed teeth.

The creature let out a bloodcurdling shriek, and Sarah screamed, dropping the bookend and stumbling back. She turned and fled, her heart pounding in her ears. She raced down the hallway, the creature's shrieks echoing behind her.

Sarah burst out of the manor and into the night, the cool air stinging her lungs. She didn't stop running until she reached her car, fumbling with the keys in her panic. Finally, she managed to unlock the car and scramble inside, slamming the door behind her.

She sat there, gasping for breath, her body trembling. She had seen something truly horrifying, something that defied explanation. But as she looked back at the manor, silhouetted against the moonlit sky, a strange feeling of fascination mingled with her fear. She had glimpsed the darkness within Blackwood Manor, and she knew she couldn't leave until she uncovered its secrets.

**(To be continued...)**

# CHAPTER THREE

# THE WHISPERING WALLS

Sarah's heart hammered against her ribs as she sprinted away from the manor, the creature's shrieks echoing in her ears. The forest seemed to close in around her, the darkness alive with unseen eyes and rustling shadows. She didn't stop running until she reached the clearing where she had parked her car. Fumbling with the keys, she managed to unlock the door and scramble inside, slamming it shut behind her as if to seal out the horrors she had just witnessed.

Gasping for breath, she slumped against the steering wheel, her body trembling with fear and adrenaline. She had seen something truly monstrous, something that defied explanation. But even as she tried to convince herself it was all a hallucination, a trick of the light, a deep, unsettling feeling told her that what she had seen was real.

As she caught her breath, her gaze drifted back towards the manor, its silhouette looming against the moonlit sky like a predatory beast. A strange mix of terror and fascination warred within her. She had glimpsed the darkness that lurked within Blackwood Manor, and a part of her, the writer, the seeker of truth, couldn't turn away.

With a shuddering breath, Sarah started the car and turned it around, heading back towards the manor. She couldn't leave, not now. She had to know what secrets lay hidden within those walls, what horrors awaited her in the depths of that ancient house.

As she approached the manor again, she noticed a faint light flickering in one of the upstairs windows. It was a small, inviting beacon in the otherwise oppressive darkness. With a renewed sense of determination, Sarah parked the car and made her way back towards the house.

This time, she entered cautiously, her senses heightened, every creak and groan of the old house setting her nerves on edge. She moved through the darkened hallways, her footsteps echoing in the eerie silence. The portraits on the walls seemed to watch her with accusing eyes, their painted faces contorted in expressions of disapproval and disdain.

As she explored the manor, she discovered a hidden passage behind a bookcase in the library. The passage was narrow and damp, the air thick with the smell of mildew and decay. Sarah hesitated, a shiver of apprehension running down her spine. But her curiosity outweighed her fear, and she pressed on, following the passage deeper into the bowels of the house.

The passage opened into a small, circular room. In the center of the room stood a stone altar, its surface etched with strange symbols and runes. A single candle burned on the altar, casting an eerie glow on the surrounding walls.

Sarah's heart pounded in her chest. She had stumbled upon something ancient and forbidden, a place where dark rituals had once been performed. She could almost feel the presence of unseen eyes upon her, the weight of centuries of secrets pressing down on her shoulders.

As she examined the altar more closely, she noticed a small, leather-bound book resting on its surface. The book was old and worn, its pages filled with faded ink and cryptic symbols. Sarah carefully opened the book, her fingers tracing the strange script.

The words were in a language she didn't recognize, but as she read, a sense of dread washed over her. The book spoke of dark magic, of summoning rituals, of ancient entities that hungered for human souls. Sarah's blood ran cold. She had stumbled upon a grimoire, a book of forbidden knowledge that should never have been found.

Suddenly, the candle on the altar flickered and went out, plunging the room into darkness. Sarah gasped, her heart pounding in her ears. She fumbled for her phone, her fingers trembling as she activated the flashlight.

The beam of light cut through the darkness, illuminating the room. But as Sarah swept the light around, she froze in terror. Standing before her, bathed in the pale glow of her phone, was the creature from the bedroom. Its eyes, black and empty, stared into her soul. Its mouth was stretched into a grotesque grin, revealing rows of razor-sharp teeth.

Sarah screamed, her voice echoing through the empty house. She stumbled back, dropping the grimoire, her mind reeling in terror. The creature lunged at her, its claws outstretched.

Sarah closed her eyes, bracing for the inevitable. But the attack never came. Instead, she heard a deafening crash, followed by a series of guttural growls and snarls.

Cautiously, Sarah opened her eyes. The creature was gone. In its place, standing protectively in front of her, was a large, shadowy figure. It was tall and imposing, its form shifting and swirling like smoke. It emitted a low growl, its eyes fixed on the spot where the creature had vanished.

Sarah stared in awe and confusion. What was this creature? Was it friend or foe? She couldn't tell, but she knew one thing: she was no longer alone in the darkness.

The shadowy figure turned its head towards Sarah, its eyes glowing with an otherworldly light. It reached out a hand towards her, its touch surprisingly gentle. Sarah hesitated, unsure whether to trust this strange being. But something in its eyes, a sense of ancient wisdom and power, compelled her to reach out and take its hand.

As their fingers touched, a jolt of energy surged through Sarah's body. She gasped, her mind flooded with images and sensations. She saw visions of the manor's past, of dark rituals and sacrifices, of the creature that haunted its halls. She felt the weight of centuries of pain and suffering, the echoes of countless souls trapped within the walls of Blackwood Manor.

And then, just as suddenly as it began, the vision ended. Sarah stumbled back, her head spinning. The shadowy figure had vanished, leaving her alone once more in the darkness. But she was no longer the same. She had seen the truth of Blackwood Manor, and she knew that her journey had just begun.

**(To be continued...)**

# CHAPTER FOUR

# THE SECRET DIARY

Sarah stood alone in the darkness, her mind reeling from the visions that had flooded her senses. The shadowy figure, the creature, the whispers of the past – it was all too much to comprehend. But one thing was clear: Blackwood Manor held secrets, dark and dangerous secrets, and she was somehow caught in the middle of them.

Determined to understand what was happening, Sarah decided to search the manor for clues. She started with the library, drawn back to the room where she had first felt a connection to the house. The shelves, packed with ancient books, seemed to beckon her closer, promising answers to the questions swirling in her mind.

As she scanned the titles, her eyes fell upon a small, leather-bound book tucked away on a high shelf. It looked old and worn, its pages yellowed with age. Curious, Sarah reached for the book, her fingers brushing against its dusty cover.

She carefully opened the book, her heart pounding with anticipation. The pages were filled with elegant handwriting, the words penned in faded ink. It was a diary, a personal account of someone's life within the walls of Blackwood Manor.

Sarah began to read, her eyes scanning the pages, her mind piecing together the story. The diary belonged to a woman named Eleanor Blackwood, who had lived in the manor centuries ago. Eleanor's entries painted a picture of a troubled soul, trapped in a loveless marriage and haunted by a sense of isolation and despair.

As Sarah read further, she discovered that Eleanor had been plagued by strange visions and nightmares, much like Sarah herself. Eleanor wrote of a darkness that lurked within the manor, a malevolent presence that whispered to her in the night, tempting her with promises of power and forbidden knowledge.

Sarah's blood ran cold as she realized that Eleanor's experiences mirrored her own. Was she destined to suffer the same fate as the long-dead woman? Was the darkness that had haunted Eleanor now reaching out to claim Sarah as its own?

Suddenly, a loud crash echoed through the house, snapping Sarah out of her thoughts. She slammed the diary shut, her heart pounding in her chest. The noise had come from upstairs, from the room where she had encountered the creature.

Fear gripped her, but curiosity pushed her forward. She had to know what was happening. Clutching the diary tightly, Sarah crept out of the library and made her way towards the staircase.

As she ascended the stairs, the feeling of being watched intensified. The whispers seemed to grow louder, the shadows deeper. Sarah felt a cold dread creeping over her, a sense of impending doom.

She reached the top of the stairs and cautiously approached the room where she had seen the creature. The door was slightly ajar, and a faint light flickered from within. Sarah took a deep breath and pushed the door open.

The room was empty. The candle on the nightstand had been knocked over, its flame extinguished, leaving the room in shadows. But as Sarah scanned the room, her eyes fell upon something that made her blood run cold.

Scrawled across the wall in what appeared to be dried blood were three words:

**"She is mine."** *

Sarah gasped, her breath catching in her throat. The message was clear, and it was terrifying. The creature, the darkness that haunted Blackwood Manor, had claimed her. And it wouldn't rest until she was its.

**(To be continued...)**

# CHAPTER FIVE

# THE GHOSTS OF BLACKWOOD

Sarah stared at the blood-red message scrawled across the wall, her mind reeling. "She is mine." The words echoed in her thoughts, a chilling reminder that she was no longer just an observer in this haunted house, but a target. The creature, whatever it was, had claimed her.

A wave of dizziness washed over her, and she stumbled back, her hand instinctively reaching out to steady herself against the wall. Her fingers brushed against something cold and smooth – a hidden door, cleverly disguised within the wood paneling.

Driven by a desperate need to escape the terrifying message and the ominous feeling that permeated the room, Sarah pushed against the hidden door. It swung inwards with a groan, revealing a narrow, dust-filled staircase leading down into the darkness.

Hesitantly, Sarah stepped onto the stairs, her phone's flashlight cutting a weak beam through the gloom. The air grew colder as she descended, heavy with the scent of damp earth and something else... something ancient and unsettling.

The staircase spiraled down into the depths of the manor, seemingly endless. Sarah's heart pounded with each step, her mind conjuring images of what horrors might await her in the darkness below.

Finally, the stairs ended at a heavy wooden door, bound in iron. Sarah pushed against it, the door creaking open to reveal a hidden chamber. The room was circular, with stone walls lined with shelves filled with strange objects – jars containing unidentifiable liquids, dried herbs hanging from the ceiling, and bizarre symbols etched into the floor.

In the center of the room stood a large, ornately carved chest. Intrigued, Sarah approached the chest, her fingers tracing the intricate patterns on its surface. She lifted the heavy lid, revealing a collection of old documents and photographs.

As she sifted through the contents, a sense of unease washed over her. The photographs were faded and yellowed, depicting people with haunted eyes and unsettling smiles. The documents were written in a language she didn't recognize, but the symbols and diagrams seemed eerily familiar, echoing the runes she had seen in the grimoire.

One photograph in particular caught her attention. It showed a group of people standing in front of the manor, their faces obscured by shadows. But in the background, Sarah could make out a figure standing near the edge of the forest. It was tall and shadowy, its form shifting and swirling like smoke. It was the same figure that had saved her from the creature.

Sarah's mind raced. Who were these people? What was their connection to the manor and the creature? And who was the shadowy figure that seemed to be both protector and prisoner of this place?

Suddenly, a cold gust of wind swept through the chamber, extinguishing her phone's light and plunging her into darkness. Sarah gasped, her heart pounding in her ears. She fumbled for her phone, desperately trying to turn the light back on.

But as she did so, she heard a whisper, close to her ear. It was a voice, ancient and chilling, speaking in a language she couldn't understand. Yet, somehow, she knew what it was saying.

"You are not alone," the voice whispered. "We are here. We have been waiting for you."

Sarah's blood ran cold. She was surrounded by unseen eyes, by the ghosts of Blackwood Manor. They were trapped here, bound to this place by some unknown force. And now, they were reaching out to her, their whispers echoing in the darkness.

Terror gripped her, and she scrambled back, her hands outstretched, searching for the door. She had to escape this chamber, this house, this place of shadows and whispers.

Just as she reached the door, a hand, cold and clammy, grasped her arm. Sarah screamed, her voice echoing through the chamber. She struggled to break free, but the grip was too strong.

She was pulled back into the darkness, the whispers growing louder, the unseen eyes closing in. Sarah felt a sense of despair wash over her. She was trapped, lost in the depths of Blackwood Manor, with no hope of escape.

And then, just as suddenly as it began, the grip loosened. Sarah stumbled forward, her hand finding the door. She flung it open and fled back up the stairs, the whispers chasing her, the ghosts of Blackwood Manor reaching out from the darkness.

She burst out of the hidden passage and into the library, gasping for breath, her body trembling. She had escaped the chamber, but she knew that the ghosts were still there, watching her, waiting for their next opportunity to claim her.

Sarah clutched the diary tightly, her mind racing. She had to find a way to break the curse that held the ghosts captive, to free them from their eternal prison. But how? And what was her connection to this place, to these people, to this darkness?

The answers, she knew, lay somewhere within the walls of Blackwood Manor. But as she looked around the darkened library, the shadows seeming to dance and whisper around her, she realized that her quest for answers had just become a fight for survival.

**(To be continued...)**

# CHAPTER SIX

# BLOODLINES

Sarah burst out of the library, the diary clutched tightly in her hand. The whispers still echoed in her ears, the unseen eyes still felt upon her. She had to get out of the manor, to escape the clutches of the darkness that seemed to permeate every corner of this ancient house.

But as she raced towards the front door, a sudden realization stopped her in her tracks. The creature, the shadowy figure, the ghosts – they all seemed connected to her somehow. The visions she had experienced, the whispers she had heard, they all hinted at a link between Sarah and Blackwood Manor, a connection she couldn't yet understand.

She turned back, her gaze drawn to the grand staircase that led to the upper floors. Something was pulling her towards those darkened rooms, a sense of urgency she couldn't ignore. She had to find answers, to uncover the truth about her connection to this place.

With renewed determination, Sarah ascended the stairs, her footsteps echoing in the eerie silence. The portraits lining the walls seemed to watch her with a mixture of curiosity and malice, their eyes following her every move.

She reached the landing and hesitated, unsure which way to go. Then, she remembered the room with the bloody message, the room where she had found the hidden passage. Perhaps there were more clues to be found there.

As she approached the room, she heard a noise from within – a soft, rhythmic tapping. Her heart pounded in her chest. Was the creature back? Or was it something else, something even more sinister?

Sarah cautiously pushed the door open, her flashlight beam cutting through the darkness. The room was empty, but the tapping continued, coming from the far corner. Sarah slowly approached the sound, her senses on high alert.

The tapping was coming from behind a large tapestry that hung on the wall. Sarah reached out and pulled the tapestry aside, revealing a small, wooden door. She hesitated, her hand hovering over the doorknob. What lay beyond this door? Another hidden chamber? Another terrifying encounter?

With a deep breath, Sarah turned the doorknob and pushed the door open. She gasped as she stepped into the room. It was a small, cozy bedroom, decorated in a feminine style. A four-poster bed draped with lace curtains dominated the room, and a vanity table with an ornate mirror stood against one wall.

But it was the objects on the nightstand that truly caught Sarah's attention. There, nestled amongst a collection of antique trinkets, was a framed photograph. Sarah picked up the photograph, her eyes widening in disbelief.

The photograph showed a young woman with dark hair and piercing blue eyes. She was strikingly beautiful, but there was something hauntingly familiar about her face. Sarah stared at the photograph, her mind racing. She knew this woman, she was sure of it. But how?

Then, it hit her. The woman in the photograph was Eleanor Blackwood, the author of the diary. But that wasn't the most shocking part. The woman in the photograph was also Sarah. Or rather, Sarah was the spitting image of her.

Sarah's mind reeled. How could this be? Was she related to Eleanor Blackwood? Was that the connection she had felt to this place, to these people?

Suddenly, a voice whispered in her ear, "You are her. You are Eleanor."

Sarah whirled around, her heart pounding in her chest. But there was no one there. The voice had come from within her own mind.

She sank onto the bed, her body trembling. The truth was out. She wasn't just connected to Eleanor Blackwood. She *was* Eleanor Blackwood. Somehow, she had been reincarnated, brought back to Blackwood Manor to relive the horrors of the past.

**(To be continued...)**

# CHAPTER SEVEN

# THE MIRROR SHOWS ALL

Sarah sat on the edge of the bed, staring at the photograph in her trembling hands. The woman in the picture, Eleanor Blackwood, was her. Or rather, she was Eleanor. The realization sent shivers down her spine, a cold wave of disbelief washing over her. Reincarnation? Was that truly possible?

She looked around the room, taking in the feminine touches, the delicate lace curtains, the ornate vanity table. This was Eleanor's room, a sanctuary where she had sought refuge from the darkness that consumed Blackwood Manor. And now, centuries later, Sarah found herself in the same room, facing the same darkness.

A sudden urge to look into the vanity mirror overcame her. She rose from the bed and approached the mirror, her heart pounding in her chest. As she gazed into its depths, she half expected to see Eleanor's reflection staring back at her.

But instead, she saw herself. Her own face, pale and drawn, her eyes wide with fear. Yet, there was something different, something unsettling about her reflection. It was as if a shadow had fallen over her features, a darkness lurking beneath the surface.

Sarah reached out and touched the mirror, her fingers tracing the outline of her reflection. As she did so, the mirror rippled, like water disturbed by a stone. The reflection distorted, twisting and shifting until it no longer resembled Sarah at all.

In her place, she saw a monstrous figure, its face contorted in a grotesque mask of rage and despair. Its eyes burned with an unholy fire, and its mouth was stretched into a wide, predatory grin, revealing rows of sharp, pointed teeth.

Sarah gasped and stumbled back, her hand flying to her mouth to stifle a scream. The creature from the bedroom, the one that had haunted her nightmares, was her. Or rather, it was a part of her, a dark side that she had never known existed.

The realization struck her like a bolt of lightning. The creature wasn't some external entity, some malevolent spirit that haunted the manor. It was her own inner darkness, her own repressed fears and anxieties given form.

And the shadowy figure, the one that had saved her from the creature, was her other half, her inner strength and resilience. The two figures, the creature and the shadow, were locked in an eternal battle within her, a struggle between light and darkness, good and evil.

Sarah sank to the floor, her mind reeling. She was the source of the darkness that plagued Blackwood Manor. She was the creature, the shadow, the ghost. She was everything.

But how could this be? How could she be both the victim and the monster? The answer, she knew, lay somewhere in her past, in the memories she had suppressed, in the secrets she had buried deep within her subconscious.

She had to unlock those memories, to confront her inner demons, to understand the darkness that resided within her. Only then could she hope to break the curse that held Blackwood Manor captive, to free the ghosts that roamed its halls, and to finally find peace.

But as she sat there, surrounded by the echoes of the past, Sarah knew that her journey had just begun. The battle within her was far from over. And the fate of Blackwood Manor, and her own soul, hung in the balance.

**(To be continued...)**

# CHAPTER EIGHT

# Trapped in Time

Sarah felt dizzy, the room spinning around her. She was Eleanor. But how? Was this a dream? A trick? Her mind struggled to grasp the truth, to make sense of the impossible.

She looked down at the diary still clutched in her hand. Eleanor's diary. Her diary. The words swam before her eyes, a jumbled mess of faded ink and frantic scribbles. She flipped through the pages, searching for answers, for some explanation of how she could be here, now, as Eleanor.

A passage caught her eye, a chilling entry dated centuries ago:

- "The mirror... it showed me the truth. I am not just Eleanor. I am more. I am bound to this place, to this time. Forever. And so will she be. She will come back, again and again, trapped in this endless cycle of horror. She will be me." *

Sarah's breath caught in her throat. Eleanor knew. She knew that Sarah would return, that they were destined to relive this nightmare over and over again. But why? What was the purpose of this endless torment?

Suddenly, the room grew cold. A gust of wind swept through the open window, sending the curtains billowing. Sarah shivered, her gaze drawn to the mirror. It seemed to pulsate with an eerie light, its surface swirling and distorting.

She couldn't resist its pull. She rose from the bed and approached the mirror, her footsteps slow and hesitant. As she gazed into its depths, she felt a strange sensation, a tugging at her consciousness, as if the mirror was trying to draw her in.

The reflection rippled, the image of her own face dissolving into a swirling vortex of colors and shapes. Sarah gasped, her hand reaching out to steady herself against the vanity table. The room spun around her, the walls closing in.

And then, everything went black.

Sarah awoke with a gasp, her body drenched in sweat. She sat up, disoriented, her heart pounding in her chest. She was no longer in Eleanor's bedroom. She was in a different room, smaller and more sparsely furnished. A single window offered a glimpse of the night sky, the moon casting an eerie glow over the unfamiliar surroundings.

She rose from the bed, her legs shaky, and approached the window. She looked out at the grounds of Blackwood Manor, the shadows stretching long and menacing in the moonlight. But something was different. The manor looked...older. More decayed. As if centuries had passed in the blink of an eye.

A wave of nausea washed over her, and she stumbled back from the window. She had to get out of this room, out of this house, out of this time. But where was she? And how had she gotten here?

She noticed a small, wooden door in the corner of the room. With trembling hands, she opened the door, revealing a narrow staircase leading upwards. She hesitated, fear gnawing at her. But she had no other choice. She had to find a way out.

She ascended the stairs, each step creaking ominously under her weight. The air grew colder as she climbed, the silence broken only by the pounding of her own heart.

The staircase led to a small attic room, filled with cobwebs and dust. A single window offered a glimpse of the moonlit sky, but the view was obscured by a thick layer of grime.

Sarah approached the window, her curiosity overcoming her fear. She wiped away the grime, peering out at the landscape below. Her breath caught in her throat.

The world outside was not the one she knew. The forest that surrounded Blackwood Manor was gone, replaced by a vast, barren wasteland. The sky was a sickly shade of green, and the air hung heavy with a sense of decay and despair.

Sarah stumbled back from the window, her mind reeling. She wasn't just trapped in Blackwood Manor. She was trapped in time. She had somehow been transported to the future, to a world ravaged by some unknown catastrophe.

And she was alone.

**(To be continued...)**

# CHAPTER NINE

# THE WASTELAND

Sarah stumbled through the wasteland, her feet sinking into the dry, cracked earth. The sky above was a sickly green, the air thick with dust and the smell of decay. Twisted metal skeletons of buildings reached towards the sky like skeletal fingers, monuments to a civilization long gone.

She didn't know how she had gotten here, how she had traveled through time. All she knew was that she was alone, stranded in a desolate future, with no way back to her own time.

Fear gnawed at her, a constant companion in this alien landscape. But beneath the fear, a spark of determination flickered. She had to survive. She had to find answers. She had to understand why she had been brought to this time, to this place.

As she wandered through the ruins, she came across a group of ragged figures huddled around a small fire. They looked up as she approached, their eyes wary and suspicious.

Sarah hesitated, unsure whether to approach them. But she was desperate for any kind of human contact, any sign that she wasn't completely alone in this desolate world.

"Hello?" she called out, her voice hoarse from disuse.

The figures exchanged glances, their expressions unreadable. One of them, a woman with a gaunt face and hollow eyes, stepped forward.

"Who are you?" she asked, her voice raspy and suspicious.

"My name is Sarah," she replied. "I... I don't know how I got here."

The woman narrowed her eyes. "You're not one of them, are you?"

"One of who?" Sarah asked, confused.

The woman gestured towards the ruins. "The creatures. The ones that haunt this place."

Sarah's heart sank. Even in this future wasteland, the darkness of Blackwood Manor had followed her. The creatures, the ghosts, they were all connected to her, bound to her by some unknown force.

"I... I think I might be," she admitted, her voice barely a whisper.

The woman's eyes widened in alarm. "Then you need to leave. Now. Before they find you."

Sarah nodded, her fear growing. But where could she go? She was lost, alone, with no way to escape this desolate future.

"Please," she begged. "Can you help me? I don't know what to do."

The woman hesitated, her gaze flickering towards the other figures huddled around the fire. They murmured amongst themselves, their voices low and urgent.

Finally, the woman turned back to Sarah. "We can't stay here. It's not safe. But there's a place, a sanctuary, where the creatures can't reach. If you come with us, we can take you there."

Sarah's heart leaped with hope. A sanctuary? A place where she could be safe from the creatures, from the darkness that haunted her? It seemed too good to be true.

But she had no other choice. She had to trust these strangers, to follow them into the unknown. Perhaps, in this desolate future, she could find a way to break the curse that bound her to Blackwood Manor, to finally escape the shadows of the past.

**(To be continued...)**

# CHAPTER TEN

# THE NIGHTMARE FACTORY

Sarah followed the group of survivors through the desolate wasteland. The sun beat down mercilessly, the air thick with dust and the stench of decay. The ruins of buildings loomed over them, their skeletal frames casting long, eerie shadows.

As they walked, Sarah couldn't shake the feeling that she was being watched. She glanced over her shoulder, but the wasteland stretched out, empty and desolate. Yet, the feeling persisted, a cold dread creeping into her heart.

The group finally reached their destination, a crumbling factory building. It was a grim place, its windows shattered and its walls scarred with graffiti. But to the survivors, it was a sanctuary, a place where they could hide from the creatures that roamed the wasteland.

Inside the factory, it was dark and cold. The air was thick with the smell of dust and decay. Sarah shivered as she followed the others through the winding corridors. The silence was broken only by the echoing footsteps and the occasional creak of the old building.

They reached a large, open room, filled with broken machinery and scattered debris. In the center of the room, a fire crackled, casting dancing shadows on the walls. The survivors gathered around the fire, their faces lit by the flames.

Sarah sat down beside one of them, a young woman named Anya. Anya had been living in the wasteland since she was a child, and she knew its dangers all too well. She told Sarah stories of the creatures, of their relentless pursuit, their insatiable hunger for human flesh.

Sarah listened, her heart pounding with fear. The creatures were not just monsters from her nightmares. They were real, terrifying beings that roamed the wasteland, hunting their prey.

As the night deepened, the temperature dropped, and the wind howled outside. Sarah huddled closer to the fire, her eyes drawn to the shadows dancing on the walls. She could have sworn she saw something move in the darkness, a flicker of movement, a glint of something sinister.

Suddenly, a bloodcurdling scream echoed through the factory. The survivors jumped to their feet, their faces etched with fear. They knew that sound. It was the cry of someone being attacked by the creatures.

Without hesitation, they grabbed their makeshift weapons and rushed towards the source of the scream. Sarah followed, her heart pounding in her chest. She had to help. She had to protect herself.

They burst into a large, open room, their flashlights illuminating the scene. The room was bathed in darkness, save for a flickering light source in the far corner. As they approached, they saw the source of the light: a creature, a monstrous abomination, its body twisted and deformed, its eyes glowing with a malevolent light.

The creature turned towards them, its mouth opening in a wide, toothy grin. It let out a blood-curdling roar, and charged at the survivors.

Sarah and the others fought back, swinging their makeshift weapons with all their might. But the creature was too strong, too fast. It tore through their defenses, its claws raking across their flesh.

One by one, the survivors fell, their screams echoing through the factory. Sarah was the only one left standing, her back pressed against the wall, her weapon raised in a defensive stance.

The creature lunged at her, its claws outstretched. Sarah closed her eyes, bracing for the inevitable. But then, something unexpected happened. A powerful force, a surge of energy, erupted from within her. She raised her hand, and a blinding light shot from her fingertips, striking the creature.

The creature let out a deafening shriek and fell to the ground, its body convulsing. The light faded, leaving Sarah standing alone in the darkness. She had defeated the creature, but at what cost?

She looked around at the carnage, the bodies of her fallen comrades scattered across the floor. A wave of grief washed over her. She had failed to protect them. She had failed to save them from the darkness that consumed this world.

But she knew she couldn't give up. There were others out there, survivors who needed her help. She had to find them, to protect them, to fight back against the darkness.

Sarah picked up the diary, the one that had led her to this terrible place. She knew that the answers she sought, the key to breaking the curse that bound her to this world, were hidden within its pages.

With renewed determination, she turned and walked back into the darkness, ready to face whatever horrors awaited her. The future was uncertain, but she was determined to fight, to survive, and to find a way back home.

# CHAPTER ELEVEN

# ECHOES OF THE PAST

Sarah wandered through the desolate wasteland, the diary clutched tightly in her hand. The world around her was a bleak and barren landscape, a stark contrast to the vibrant life she remembered. The sky was a perpetual sickly green, the air heavy with dust and the stench of decay. Twisted metal skeletons of buildings reached towards the sky like accusing fingers, remnants of a civilization long gone.

She felt a profound sense of loneliness, a chilling isolation that gnawed at her soul. The silence of the wasteland was deafening, broken only by the occasional howl of the wind and the crunch of her own footsteps on the dry, cracked earth.

She consulted the diary, hoping for some clue, some direction, some glimmer of hope in this desolate world. The faded ink spoke of Eleanor's struggles, her fears, her growing despair as she witnessed the slow decay of her world. But there were also glimpses of hope, of a hidden sanctuary, a place where the creatures couldn't reach.

Sarah clung to those words, those whispers of hope in the darkness. She had to find this sanctuary, this haven from the horrors that plagued this world. It was her only chance, her only hope for survival.

As she journeyed through the wasteland, she came across strange, shimmering portals, swirling vortexes of energy that seemed to distort the very fabric of space and time. She remembered the mirror in Eleanor's room, the way it had rippled and twisted before transporting her to this future. Were these portals connected to the mirror? Were they a way back to her own time?

Driven by a desperate hope, Sarah approached one of the portals. She reached out a hesitant hand, her fingers tingling as they neared the swirling energy. She could feel a pull, a beckoning towards the unknown.

But then, she hesitated. What lay beyond the portal? Was it a way back to her own time, or was it a trap, a gateway to something even more terrifying?

She remembered the creatures, their monstrous forms, their insatiable hunger. They were a part of her, a dark reflection of her own inner demons. Were they waiting for her on the other side of the portal?

Fear warred with hope within her. She longed to escape this desolate future, to return to her own time, to her own life. But the risk was too great. She couldn't risk falling into the clutches of the creatures, of becoming the monster she feared most.

With a heavy heart, Sarah turned away from the portal. She would continue her search for the sanctuary, for a place where she could be safe, where she could understand the darkness within her and find a way to overcome it.

As she journeyed on, she came across a group of children huddled together in the ruins of a building. They were thin and ragged, their eyes wide with fear. Sarah's heart went out to them. They were innocent victims of this desolate world, caught in the crossfire of a battle they didn't understand.

She approached them cautiously, offering them what little food and water she had left. The children looked at her with suspicion at first, but their hunger overcame their fear, and they gratefully accepted her offering.

As Sarah spoke to them, she learned that they had lost their families to the creatures, that they were alone and afraid. Sarah felt a surge of protectiveness towards them. She couldn't abandon them to this harsh world.

She decided to take them with her, to find the sanctuary together. Perhaps, in protecting these children, she could find a way to redeem herself, to atone for the darkness within her.

As they journeyed together, Sarah felt a glimmer of hope rekindle within her. She was no longer alone. She had a purpose, a reason to fight. And she knew, deep down, that she would find a way to overcome the darkness, to break the curse, and to return to her own time.

**(To be continued...)**

# CHAPTER TWELVE

# THE SANCTUARY

Sarah and the children trudged through the wasteland, their footsteps muffled by the thick dust that blanketed the ground. The sun beat down mercilessly, the air hot and dry. Sarah could feel the children's exhaustion, their small bodies struggling to keep up with her pace.

But she couldn't stop. They had to reach the sanctuary before nightfall. Anya had warned her about the creatures that roamed the wasteland after dark, their hunger insatiable, their forms shifting and terrifying.

As the sun began to dip below the horizon, casting long shadows across the desolate landscape, Sarah spotted a faint light in the distance. Hope surged through her. Could it be the sanctuary?

She quickened her pace, the children trailing behind her. As they drew closer, the light grew brighter, revealing a cluster of buildings nestled within a rocky outcrop. It was a small settlement, a haven of life in the vast emptiness of the wasteland.

Sarah and the children approached cautiously, their eyes scanning the surroundings for any sign of danger. But the settlement seemed peaceful, the only sound the gentle murmur of voices and the crackling of fires.

As they entered the settlement, they were greeted by a group of people, their faces etched with curiosity and cautious welcome. Sarah explained their situation, how they had been wandering through the wasteland, seeking refuge from the creatures.

The people of the sanctuary listened intently, their expressions growing somber as Sarah recounted her experiences. When she finished, an elderly woman stepped forward, her eyes filled with wisdom and compassion.

"You are welcome here, Sarah," she said. "We have been expecting you."

Sarah's heart skipped a beat. Expecting her? How could they have known she was coming?

The woman smiled gently. "We have seen you in our dreams, Sarah. We know of your struggles, of the darkness that haunts you. We are here to help you."

Sarah felt a wave of relief wash over her. Finally, she had found a place where she was not alone, where people understood her burden and were willing to help her carry it.

The people of the sanctuary welcomed Sarah and the children with open arms. They provided them with food, shelter, and a sense of community that Sarah had longed for. She felt a sense of belonging, a feeling of hope that she hadn't experienced since entering this desolate future.

As she settled into her new surroundings, Sarah learned more about the sanctuary and its inhabitants. They were a group of survivors, people who had managed to escape the creatures and build a new life in the wasteland. They had learned to harness the power of the portals, using them to travel to different times and dimensions, gathering knowledge and resources to help them survive.

Sarah was fascinated by their stories, by their resilience and their determination to create a better future. She felt a renewed sense of purpose, a desire to contribute to their community, to use her own experiences to help them in their fight against the darkness.

But she couldn't shake the feeling that there was more to her presence in the sanctuary, that her arrival had been foretold for a reason. She had to uncover the truth about her connection to Blackwood Manor, to the creatures, to this desolate future.

And she knew that the answers lay somewhere within the diary, within the words of Eleanor Blackwood, the woman who was both her past and her present.

**(To be continued...)**

# CHAPTER THIRTEEN

# JOURNEY INTO DARKNESS

Sarah delved deeper into the diary, the worn leather binding cool to the touch. The pages crackled as she turned them, each one revealing a chilling piece of Eleanor's story. She learned about the ancient rituals, the dark powers that had corrupted the manor, and the terrifying creatures that lurked in the shadows.

One entry, in particular, caught her attention. It spoke of a secret room, a place of power, where the true evil resided. Eleanor had warned of the dangers of this place, of the horrors that awaited those who dared to enter.

Intrigued and terrified, Sarah decided to seek out this hidden room. With the help of the sanctuary's elders, she deciphered the clues hidden within the diary, leading her to a forgotten wing of the manor.

The journey was perilous, filled with traps and dark secrets. Sarah and her companions navigated through shadowy corridors, dodged hidden pitfalls, and evaded the watchful eyes of the creatures that lurked in the shadows.

Finally, they reached the hidden room. It was a circular chamber, its walls adorned with strange symbols and grotesque carvings. In the center of the room, a dark, swirling portal pulsed with an otherworldly energy.

As Sarah approached the portal, a sense of dread washed over her. She could feel the darkness emanating from it, a malevolent force that threatened to consume her. But she was determined to face her fears, to confront the darkness within herself.

With a trembling hand, Sarah reached out and touched the portal. The moment her fingers made contact, the world around her dissolved, and she was pulled into the swirling vortex.

She found herself in a nightmarish landscape, a place of eternal darkness and suffering. Twisted, monstrous creatures roamed the land, their eyes glowing with a malevolent light. They were the embodiment of the darkness that had plagued Blackwood Manor, the creatures that had haunted her dreams.

Sarah was alone, lost in this hellish realm. She fought desperately to survive, using her knowledge of the creatures' weaknesses, the lessons she had learned from the diary. But it was a losing battle. The creatures were relentless, their numbers seemingly endless.

As she was cornered by a particularly monstrous creature, Sarah felt a surge of despair. She was about to meet her end, to become one of the creatures herself.

Then, she remembered the words of the sanctuary elders, the ancient wisdom they had passed down through generations. She focused her mind, channeling her inner strength, and called upon the power of light.

A blinding light erupted from her, pushing back the darkness. The creature recoiled, its form dissolving into shadows. Sarah was surrounded by a protective aura, shielding her from the darkness.

She realized then that the power to defeat the darkness lay within her, in her ability to harness the light within her soul. She was not just a victim of fate; she was a warrior, a protector of light in a world consumed by darkness.

With renewed determination, Sarah faced the creatures, her light sword cutting through the darkness. She fought with a ferocity she never knew she possessed, her every move a testament to her growing strength.

One by one, the creatures fell before her, their forms dissolving into nothingness. The darkness began to recede, the nightmarish landscape fading away.

Sarah found herself back in the hidden chamber, the portal now dormant. She was exhausted, but she felt a sense of triumph. She had faced the darkness within herself, and she had emerged victorious.

As she stepped out of the chamber, she knew that her journey was far from over. The battle against the darkness was eternal, and she was destined to be its champion. She would return to the wasteland, to protect the survivors, to fight for a future free from the clutches of the darkness.

And so, Sarah continued her quest, armed with the knowledge of the past and the power of the future. She was the light in the darkness, the hope in the despair. And she would not rest until the darkness was banished, and the world was restored to its rightful balance.

# CHAPTER FOURTEEN

# THE GATHERING STORM

News of Sarah's victory against the creatures spread quickly through the sanctuary. The survivors, who had long lived in fear of the darkness, now saw a glimmer of hope. Sarah, the woman who had emerged from the past, the woman who could wield the power of light, was their champion, their protector.

But Sarah knew that the battle was far from over. The creatures were relentless, their numbers vast. And the darkness that spawned them, the evil that had corrupted Blackwood Manor, still lurked in the shadows, waiting for its chance to strike.

She spent her days training with the sanctuary's elders, learning to harness her newfound powers, to control the light that flowed through her. She practiced wielding her light sword, its blade shimmering with a radiant energy that could banish the creatures back to the shadows.

She also continued to study the diary, searching for clues about the nature of the darkness, the origins of the creatures, and the key to breaking the curse that bound her to this desolate future.

One day, while meditating in the sanctuary's central chamber, Sarah experienced a vision. She saw a swirling vortex of darkness, a portal opening in the heart of the wasteland. From this portal, a horde of creatures emerged, their numbers greater than any she had seen before.

She also saw a figure standing amidst the creatures, a figure cloaked in shadows, its eyes glowing with a malevolent light. It was the leader of the creatures, the source of their power, the embodiment of the darkness that plagued this world.

Sarah awoke from the vision with a start, her heart pounding in her chest. She knew that the vision was a warning, a premonition of a coming storm. The creatures were gathering their forces, preparing for a final assault on the sanctuary.

She shared her vision with the elders, and a sense of urgency gripped the community. They knew they had to prepare for the coming battle, to defend their sanctuary against the forces of darkness.

The survivors worked tirelessly, fortifying their defenses, gathering weapons, and training for combat. Sarah led the training sessions, sharing her knowledge of the creatures' weaknesses, teaching them how to harness their own inner strength to fight back against the darkness.

As the days passed, the tension in the sanctuary grew. The air crackled with anticipation, the silence broken only by the clang of weapons and the murmurs of worried voices.

Then, one night, the storm broke. The ground trembled, and a dark cloud descended over the sanctuary, blocking out the sickly green sky. From the heart of the cloud, a swirling vortex of darkness emerged, the portal from Sarah's vision.

The creatures poured forth from the portal, their numbers overwhelming, their forms grotesque and terrifying. They swarmed towards the sanctuary, their eyes glowing with a hunger for destruction.

The battle began. The survivors fought bravely, their weapons flashing in the darkness. Sarah stood at the forefront, her light sword a beacon of hope against the encroaching shadows.

But the creatures were relentless, their attacks fierce and unrelenting. The survivors fell one by one, their cries of pain echoing through the night.

Sarah fought with all her might, her light sword cutting through the darkness, banishing the creatures back to the shadows. But she was outnumbered, overwhelmed. She could feel her strength waning, her hope fading.

Just as she was about to succumb to the darkness, a figure emerged from the shadows. It was the shadowy figure, the one who had saved her from the creature in the manor. It stood beside her, its eyes glowing with an otherworldly light.

Together, they fought back against the creatures, their combined power a force to be reckoned with. The tide of the battle began to turn, the creatures faltering, their attacks weakening.

But then, the leader of the creatures emerged from the portal. It was a monstrous being, its form shifting and swirling, its eyes burning with a malevolent light. It raised its hand, and a wave of darkness washed over the battlefield, engulfing Sarah and the shadowy figure.

Sarah cried out as the darkness enveloped her, its icy grip chilling her to the bone. She felt her strength draining away, her light fading. She was losing the battle, losing herself to the darkness.

(To be continued...)

45

# CHAPTER FIFTEEN

# LIGHT'S FURY

The darkness pressed down on Sarah, suffocating, icy, and filled with the creature's triumphant laughter. It felt like her very essence was being pulled apart, her connection to the light flickering like a dying candle. But somewhere deep inside, a spark of defiance ignited. She wouldn't let the darkness win, not after coming this far.

With a surge of willpower, Sarah summoned the light within her. It burst forth, a blinding wave that pushed back the oppressive shadows. The creature roared in anger, its voice a guttural growl that shook the very foundations of the sanctuary.

Sarah's light sword blazed with renewed intensity, its energy cutting through the darkness like a beacon of hope. She lunged at the creature, her movements fueled by a desperate fury. The creature, surprised by her sudden resurgence, stumbled back, its shadowy form flickering.

The battle raged. Sarah, empowered by the light, fought with a ferocity she never knew she possessed. She parried the creature's attacks, her light sword deflecting its claws with a shower of sparks. Each strike she landed sent shockwaves through the creature's form, its shadowy body dissolving and reforming in a desperate attempt to withstand the onslaught.

The survivors, witnessing Sarah's fierce determination, rallied. They fought with renewed vigor, their weapons finding their marks with greater accuracy. The tide of the battle began to turn.

But the creature, sensing its impending defeat, unleashed a wave of pure darkness, a suffocating wave that threatened to extinguish the light and consume everything in its path. Sarah cried out, the darkness seeping into her, chilling her to the bone.

Just as she felt her strength waning, a familiar presence materialized beside her. The shadowy figure, its eyes glowing with an otherworldly light, joined the fray. Together, they pushed back against the encroaching darkness, their combined power a force to be reckoned with.

The shadowy figure moved with a speed and grace that defied description, its attacks a blur of motion. It weaved through the creatures, its touch leaving trails of dissipating shadows in its wake. With each strike, the creatures' forms grew weaker, their power diminishing.

Sarah, inspired by the shadowy figure's strength, focused her own power. She channeled the light within her, her sword becoming a conduit for its radiant energy. With a final, powerful swing, she struck the creature, its form shattering into a million pieces.

The darkness that had enveloped the sanctuary lifted, the light returning in a triumphant wave. The remaining creatures, their leader vanquished, fled back through the portal, their howls of defeat echoing through the wasteland.

Sarah and the shadowy figure stood side-by-side, their combined power having saved the sanctuary from the brink of destruction. But as the portal began to close, Sarah felt a strange pull, a sense of urgency that she couldn't ignore.

She knew she had to go back, to face the darkness at its source, to break the cycle that had bound her and Eleanor to Blackwood Manor for centuries. She turned to the shadowy figure, her heart heavy with gratitude and a newfound understanding.

"Thank you," she whispered. "For everything."

The shadowy figure nodded, its eyes filled with a deep sadness. "The darkness is not easily defeated, Sarah. But the light within you is strong. Use it wisely."

With a final farewell, Sarah stepped towards the closing portal. As she was pulled through the swirling vortex, she glanced back at the sanctuary, at the survivors who had become her family, at the wasteland that had become her temporary home.

She knew that her journey was far from over. But she also knew that she was not alone. The light within her, the strength she had found in this desolate future, would guide her path. She would return to Blackwood Manor, to confront the darkness at its source, and finally break free from the shadows of the past.

# CHAPTER SIXTEEN

# THE CYCLE REPEATS

Sarah emerged from the swirling vortex, her body aching and her mind reeling. She found herself back in the familiar surroundings of Blackwood Manor, the eerie silence broken only by the ticking of the grandfather clock.

She looked around, her eyes scanning the room. Everything seemed the same, yet different. The dust-covered furniture, the faded tapestries, the portraits of long-dead ancestors – all held a sense of familiarity, yet also a chilling strangeness.

Sarah knew she had to find Eleanor's diary. It held the key to understanding the darkness that plagued the manor, the key to breaking the cycle of suffering. She searched the room, her fingers tracing the dust-covered surfaces of furniture and bookshelves.

Finally, she found it, hidden beneath a loose floorboard. The diary, worn and tattered, lay open to a page filled with Eleanor's frantic handwriting. The words danced before her eyes, a chilling tale of despair and desperation.

Eleanor had written about the creature, the one that had tormented her for centuries. It was a creature of pure darkness, a manifestation of fear and hatred. It fed on the souls of the living, trapping them in an eternal cycle of suffering.

Eleanor had also written about the mirror, the gateway to another dimension, a place where the creature could draw its power. She had warned Sarah about the mirror, the dangers it posed, the darkness it could unleash.

Sarah closed the diary, her mind racing. She had to destroy the mirror, to sever the creature's connection to this world. But how? The mirror was powerful, its magic ancient and potent.

She decided to seek help from the sanctuary elders. They were wise and powerful, with knowledge beyond her comprehension. Perhaps they could offer a solution, a way to defeat the creature and break the curse.

With the diary in hand, Sarah returned to the wasteland, to the sanctuary. The survivors were overjoyed to see her, their faces lit with hope. They had missed her, her guidance, her strength.

Sarah shared her discovery with the elders, the revelation that she was Eleanor, reincarnated to break the curse. The elders listened intently, their faces grave. They confirmed that the mirror was indeed a powerful artifact, a gateway to the darkness.

To destroy the mirror, Sarah would need to confront her deepest fears, to face the darkness within herself. The elders offered their guidance, their wisdom, their power. They would help her, but the ultimate battle would be hers alone.

Sarah was ready. She was prepared to face the darkness, to break the cycle, to free herself and the manor from the clutches of the creature. With the support of the sanctuary and the wisdom of the elders, she would emerge victorious.

# CHAPTER SEVENTEEN

# WHISPERS OF THE PAST

The sanctuary bustled with activity. Survivors went about their daily tasks, repairing structures, tending to crops, and training for combat. But an undercurrent of anxiety ran through the community. The recent attack had shaken them, a stark reminder of the ever-present danger lurking just beyond their walls.

Sarah, despite her exhaustion from the battle, couldn't rest. Eleanor's diary weighed heavily in her pocket, a constant reminder of the darkness that awaited her back at Blackwood Manor. The elders had given her guidance, but the task ahead felt daunting. She was, after all, facing an ancient evil, a force that had haunted the Blackwood lineage for centuries.

She sought out the eldest of the elders, a woman named Elara, whose wisdom and knowledge were revered throughout the sanctuary. Elara, with her kind eyes and gentle demeanor, had become a source of comfort and guidance for Sarah.

"Elara," Sarah began, her voice filled with uncertainty, "I'm ready to return to the manor, to face the darkness. But

I'm afraid. What if I'm not strong enough?"

Elara smiled reassuringly. "Sarah, the light within you is stronger than you realize. You have faced the creatures, you have protected this sanctuary. You have the power to break the cycle."

"But the mirror..." Sarah said, her voice trembling, "Eleanor warned about its power. How can I possibly destroy it?"

Elara placed a comforting hand on Sarah's shoulder. "The mirror is a gateway, Sarah, a conduit for the darkness. But it is also a reflection. It shows us our deepest fears, our hidden truths. To destroy the mirror, you must first confront the darkness within yourself."

Sarah nodded slowly, her mind grappling with Elara's words. She had faced the creatures, the physical manifestations of the darkness. But the true battle, the one that would determine her fate and the fate of Blackwood Manor, lay within her own soul.

Elara continued, "The diary holds the key, Sarah. Eleanor's words will guide you. She faced the darkness, just as you are doing now. Her experiences, her struggles, her wisdom – they are all there, waiting to be discovered."

Sarah clutched the diary tighter, her resolve strengthening. She would face her fears, she would confront the darkness, and she would break the cycle. For herself, for Eleanor, and for all those who had been trapped in the shadows of Blackwood Manor.

With a renewed sense of purpose, Sarah prepared for her return to the manor. The elders gathered around her, offering their blessings and their support. They knew the dangers she faced, but they also knew that she was their only hope.

As Sarah stepped through the portal, back into the desolate world of Blackwood Manor, she carried the weight of their hopes and the burden of her destiny. The battle ahead would be the greatest challenge she had ever faced, but she was ready. She was Eleanor, and she was Sarah. And she would not rest until the darkness was vanquished, and the cycle was broken.

# CHAPTER EIGHTEEN

# FACING THE SHADOWS

Sarah stepped back into the decaying grandeur of Blackwood Manor. Dust motes danced in the shafts of pale sunlight that filtered through the grimy windows, illuminating the cobwebs and faded tapestries that adorned the once-opulent rooms. The silence was heavy, broken only by the creaking of floorboards and the distant ticking of the grandfather clock.

Clutching Eleanor's diary, Sarah felt a strange sense of déjà vu. She had been here before, not just in this lifetime, but in countless others, trapped in an endless cycle of horror. But this time, she was determined to break free.

She made her way to the library, drawn by the promise of knowledge and answers hidden within the countless volumes that lined the shelves. The room was dark and musty, the air thick with the smell of decaying paper and forgotten stories.

Sarah lit a candle, its flickering flame casting dancing shadows on the walls. She sat down at a dusty table, the diary open before her. Eleanor's words, penned centuries ago, seemed to whisper to her, guiding her towards the truth.

The diary spoke of the creature's origins, of a dark ritual that had corrupted the manor and unleashed a malevolent force into the world. It spoke of the mirror, a gateway to another dimension, a place where the creature drew its power.

Sarah shivered as she read, her heart pounding with a mixture of fear and determination. She had to find a way to destroy the mirror, to sever the creature's connection to this world. But how?

She remembered Elara's words: "To destroy the mirror, you must first confront the darkness within yourself."

Sarah closed her eyes, taking a deep breath. She had to delve into her own past, into the darkest corners of her soul, to find the strength to face the creature.

She thought back to her childhood, to the fears and anxieties that had haunted her. She remembered the feeling of being different, of not belonging, of being trapped in a world that didn't understand her.

She thought about her struggles as a writer, the self-doubt, the fear of failure, the constant pressure to prove herself. She remembered the disappointment of her first book, the harsh criticism, the feeling of being a failure.

And then, she thought about the wasteland, the desolate future she had witnessed, the creatures that roamed the land, the survivors who had lost everything. She remembered the fear, the despair, the overwhelming sense of hopelessness.

But she also remembered the strength she had found within herself, the power of the light, the courage to fight back against the darkness. She remembered the sanctuary, the community of survivors, the hope that they had given her.

Sarah opened her eyes, a newfound determination burning within her. She had faced her shadows, the darkness within herself. And she had found the light, the strength to overcome it.

She rose from the table, the diary clutched tightly in her hand. She knew what she had to do. She would confront the creature, she would destroy the mirror, and she would break the cycle.

She made her way to the hidden room, the place where the mirror resided. The air grew colder as she approached, the silence heavier. She could feel the creature's presence, its malevolent energy radiating from the room.

Sarah took a deep breath and pushed the door open. The room was dark, the only light coming from the faint glow of the mirror. It hung on the wall, its surface swirling with shadows, its depths beckoning her closer.

Sarah approached the mirror, her heart pounding in her chest. She could see her reflection, her face pale and determined. But she could also see something else, a darkness lurking beneath the surface, a shadow that mirrored the creature's form.

Sarah knew that this was the final battle, the culmination of her journey. She had to face the darkness within herself, to conquer the creature that had haunted her for centuries.

She raised her hand, her light sword glowing with a radiant energy. She was ready. She was Eleanor. She was Sarah. And she would not be defeated.

# CHAPTER NINETEEN

# SHATTERED REFLECTIONS

The air crackled with tension as Sarah stood before the mirror, its surface a swirling vortex of shadows and whispers. The creature's presence was overwhelming, a suffocating weight that pressed down on her, threatening to consume her. But Sarah held her ground, her gaze unwavering, her resolve unshakeable.

She had journeyed through time, faced her deepest fears, and confronted the darkness within herself. She had learned to harness the power of light, to wield it as a weapon against the shadows that had haunted her for centuries. And now, she was ready to face the creature, to break the cycle of suffering that had plagued Blackwood Manor for generations.

"I am not afraid of you," she declared, her voice ringing out in the silence of the hidden chamber. "I am not your victim. I am not your prisoner. I am free."

The creature's laughter echoed through the manor, a chilling sound that sent shivers down her spine. "You cannot escape me, Sarah," it hissed, its voice a venomous whisper that slithered through the air. "We are bound together, you and I. We are one."

"No," Sarah retorted, her voice firm and resolute. "We are not one. I am Sarah. And I am stronger than you."

She raised her light sword, its blade ablaze with a radiant energy that defied the encroaching darkness. The creature lunged at her, its form a grotesque distortion of shadow and rage. But Sarah was ready. She parried its attack, her sword deflecting its claws with a shower of sparks.

The battle raged, a clash of light and darkness, of good and evil. Sarah fought with a ferocity she had never known before, her movements fluid and precise, her strikes fueled by a righteous anger that burned within her soul.

The creature, surprised by her strength and determination, faltered. Its attacks grew less frequent, its movements less sure. Sarah pressed her advantage, her light sword a beacon of hope against the encroaching shadows.

With a powerful swing, she struck the creature, its form dissolving into a swirling vortex of darkness. The creature shrieked in agony, its voice echoing through the manor, a sound of despair and defeat.

Sarah didn't relent. She continued her assault, her sword a whirlwind of light, each strike chipping away at the creature's power. The mirror, the source of the creature's strength, began to crack and splinter under the strain.

With a final, decisive blow, Sarah shattered the mirror. The fragments scattered across the floor, reflecting the fading remnants of the creature's form. A wave of energy pulsed through the manor, the darkness receding like a tide, the shadows retreating back into the corners.

The creature's laughter, once so menacing, now a whimper of despair, faded into silence. The air grew lighter, the oppressive weight lifting from Sarah's shoulders. She had done it. She had defeated the creature, broken the cycle, and freed Blackwood Manor from the clutches of darkness.

But as the last vestiges of the creature's presence dissipated, a new sensation washed over Sarah. It wasn't the triumphant joy she had expected, but a strange emptiness, a void where the creature's darkness had once resided.

She realized then that the creature had been a part of her, a dark reflection of her own fears and anxieties. And now that it was gone, a part of her felt missing, incomplete.

She looked at the shattered fragments of the mirror, each one reflecting a distorted image of herself. She saw the fear, the doubt, the darkness that had haunted her for so long. But she also saw the strength, the courage, the light that had allowed her to overcome it all.

Sarah knew that the battle against the darkness was not over. It would always be a part of her, a shadow lurking in the depths of her soul. But she also knew that she had the power to control it, to keep it at bay.

She had found the light within herself, and she would never let it go out. She would carry it with her, a beacon of hope in a world that often seemed shrouded in darkness.

As she stood amidst the shattered remnants of the mirror, Sarah felt a sense of peace she had never known before. She was free. Free from the creature, free from the cycle, free from the shadows of the past.

But as she turned to leave the hidden chamber, a new question arose in her mind. What now? What would she do with her newfound freedom? Where would she go?

The answer, she knew, lay within her heart. She would return to the sanctuary, to the community of survivors who had become her family. She would use her power, her light, to help them rebuild their lives, to create a better future in the wasteland.

And perhaps, one day, she would find a way to return to her own time, to share her story, to warn others about the darkness that lurked within Blackwood Manor, and to inspire them to find the light within themselves.

But for now, she would savor her victory, the hard-won freedom that she had fought so hard to achieve. She had faced the shadows, and she had emerged victorious. And that was enough.

# CHAPTER TWENTY

# A New Dawn (and a Looming Shadow)

But the woman was powerful, her darkness a formidable force. Sarah felt her strength waning, her light flickering under the onslaught. Just as she felt herself faltering, the shadowy figure, with a surge of power, shoved Sarah towards the portal.

"Go!" it commanded, its voice echoing with urgency. "She is not your fight, not yet. Warn your world. Prepare them. I will hold her back."

Before Sarah could protest, the portal's pull intensified, dragging her towards its swirling depths. She caught one last glimpse of the shadowy figure, its form flickering as it battled the woman, its eyes filled with a deep sadness.

"No!" Sarah cried out, reaching for the figure, but it was too late. The portal consumed her, the wasteland fading away as she was hurled back through time.

She landed with a thud on the dusty floor of Blackwood Manor, the familiar silence now deafening after the chaos of the battle. The shattered remnants of the mirror lay scattered around her, a reminder of her victory against the creature.

But there was no time to celebrate. The woman's chilling words echoed in her mind: "The game has just begun."

Sarah knew that the darkness had not been defeated, merely delayed. A new threat had emerged, a new enemy with powers beyond anything she had ever encountered. And the shadowy figure, her protector, her guide, was now trapped in the wasteland, facing that threat alone.

A wave of fear washed over her, but it was quickly replaced by a steely determination. She would not let the shadowy figure's sacrifice be in vain. She would warn her world, prepare them for the coming darkness. And she would find a way to return to the wasteland, to help the sanctuary, to stand beside the shadowy figure once more.

But first, she had to understand the woman, her powers, her motives. Who was she? Where did she come from? And why was she so determined to unleash darkness upon the world?

Sarah clutched Eleanor's diary, its worn pages offering a glimmer of hope. Perhaps within its secrets, she would find the answers she sought, the key to defeating the new darkness and saving both her worlds.

As she stepped out of the hidden chamber, leaving behind the shattered remnants of the past, Sarah looked towards the future, her eyes filled with a mix of apprehension and resolve. The battle was far from over. The game had just begun.

**(The End... for now. But the story continues...)**

# Author's Note

The seeds of "The Shadow in the Blackwood Mirror" were planted in my childhood, in the long, dark hours spent hiding under the covers, my imagination conjuring terrifying creatures and haunted houses. Those childhood fears, though faded, never truly left me, and they eventually found their way onto the pages of this book.

Writing this story was a journey of confronting my own shadows, of exploring the darkness that lurks within us all. But it was also a journey of discovery, of finding the strength and resilience of the human spirit, even in the face of overwhelming fear.

I hope that this book will resonate with readers who have also faced their own demons, who have struggled with self-doubt and anxiety. May it serve as a reminder that we are not alone in our battles, that there is always light to be found, even in the darkest of times.

I would like to express my gratitude to the incredible community of beta readers and editors who provided invaluable feedback and support throughout the writing process. Your insights and encouragement helped shape this story into what it is today.

And to my readers, thank you for joining me on this journey into the shadows. I hope you'll stay tuned for the next chapter in Sarah's story, as she faces new challenges and confronts an even greater darkness.

# About The Author

Gaurav Chandrawanshi is an 18-year-old writer with a passion for horror and a gift for weaving chilling tales. "The Shadow in the Blackwood Mirror" marks his thrilling debut in the world of fiction, a dark and captivating story that will leave you breathless. But Gaurav's creativity doesn't stop there – he's also a poet, with his first collection, "I Wrote Your Name and Called it a Poetry, But in the End, I Finally Found Myself," due for release soon. This introspective collection explores themes of self-discovery, love, loss, and the challenges of navigating the complexities of life.

Beyond his writing, Gaurav is a multifaceted individual with a deep fascination for the cosmos. An avid astrophile, he finds inspiration in the vastness of space and the mysteries it holds. His love for music is evident in his songwriting and piano playing, adding another layer to his artistic expression.

When he's not crafting spine-tingling stories or soul-stirring poetry, Gaurav can be found exploring abandoned buildings (strictly during daylight hours!), collecting vintage horror movie posters, and indulging in copious amounts of coffee.

Connect with Gaurav online:

Email: gauravchandrawanshi@icloud.com

Instagram: @Gauravchandrawanshiii

Instagram: @gauravthepoet

Instagram: @gauravchandrawanshimusic

www.ingramcontent.com/pod-product-compliance
Lightning Source LLC
Chambersburg PA
CBHW031330130726
47988CB00007B/3067